PJMASKS
Owlette
Gets a Pet

Based on the episode "Owlette's Feathered Friend"

SIMON SPOTLIGHT
An imprint of Simon & Schuster Children's Publishing Division
New York London Toronto Sydney New Delhi
1230 Avenue of the Americas, New York, New York 10020
This Simon Spotlight paperback edition December 2017
This book is based on the TV series PJ MASKS © Frog Box / Entertainment One UK Limited / Walt Disney EMEA Productions Limited 2014;
Les Pyjamasques by Romuald © (2007) Gallimard Jeunnesse. All Rights Reserved.
This book/publication © Entertainment One UK Limited 2017.
Adapted by Maggie Testa from the series PJ Masks
All rights reserved, including the right of reproduction in whole or in part in any form.
SIMON SPOTLIGHT and colophon are registered trademarks of Simon & Schuster, Inc.
For information about special discounts for bulk purchases, please contact
Simon & Schuster Special Sales at 1-866-506-1949 or business@simonandschuster.com.
Manufactured in the United States of America 1217 LAK
2 3 4 5 6 7 8 9 10 • ISBN 978-1-5344-1049-7 (pbk) • ISBN 978-1-5344-1050-3 (eBook)

Amaya and Connor are playing at Greg's house when Greg shows them his pet lizard, Lionel.

"I wish I had a pet," says Amaya. "They're lots of fun."

"Yeah, but they're hard work, too," says Greg.

Amaya smiles. "I guess, but they're *mostly* fun!"

All of a sudden, the friends' bracelets start to flash and buzz.
"It's the alarm signal. Someone's trying to break into HQ!" says Greg.
"PJ Masks, we're on our way! Into the night to save the day!" they all say.

Amaya becomes Owlette!

Connor becomes Catboy!

Greg becomes Gekko!

The intruder isn't a baddie. It's a bird, and Owlette decides it will be her new pet, Birdy! Gekko reminds her that pets are a lot of work, but Owlette isn't worried.

The PJ Masks have no idea that Luna Girl is spying on them with her magical Luna Magnet and wants to teach Owlette a lesson.

Then Gekko notices something on the PJ Picture Player: Luna Girl is taking a vase from the museum, and she is getting away!

"You stay with Birdy," Catboy tells Owlette. "Gekko and I will deal with Luna Girl."

"But I want to come on the mission," says Owlette. "I'm sure Birdy will be fine."

The heroes zoom out of HQ in Owlette's Owl-Glider, catch up to Luna Girl, and return the vase to the museum.

The PJ Masks have no idea that, back at HQ, Birdy is following orders from Luna Girl, who trained her to place a Luna Crystal in the room. A Luna Beam is shooting out!

When the PJ Masks return, HQ is a mess!

"Birdy, why did you do this?" cries Owlette.

"Maybe because you left her alone," suggests Gekko. "Lionel always makes a mess when I don't pay enough attention to him. Pets are fun, but they need exercise and training and lots of . . ."

Gekko is interrupted by the PJ Picture Player's alarm.
"Luna Girl is at the zoo," says Owlette, and they run toward the exit.
"What about Birdy?" Gekko asks Owlette.
Owlette has an idea. "She can come too. I'll train her as we go!"
Gekko does not think that is a good idea at all!

The heroes find that Luna Girl let the butterflies out of their enclosure! The PJ Masks have to get the butterflies back inside, but Birdy keeps scaring them away, so Owlette puts her in the Owl-Glider.

"Birdy only wants some attention," Gekko tells Owlette.

Meanwhile, Luna Girl places two Luna Crystals in Birdy's wings to bring back to HQ so Luna Girl can take control of it.

Once the PJ Masks are finished saving the butterflies, they head back to HQ and notice that Birdy is hungry.

Owlette takes Birdy up to her room to give her some food, but then Luna Girl appears on the Owl Eye screen. Owlette decides to wait to feed Birdy. Right now she has to stop Luna Girl!

While the PJ Masks are gone from HQ, Birdy plants the two Luna Crystals, and purple Luna Beams shoot out of HQ's Owl Eyes. Soon all kinds of things start flying toward HQ!

"I've turned HQ into a giant Luna Magnet," Luna Girl explains. "Thanks to that bird, it'll pull in everything in the city till it's all mine!"

Owlette knows that if she had trained, fed, and paid attention to Birdy, this wouldn't have happened.

She turns to Birdy. "Birdy, I promise I won't let you down again. I'll build you a nest and feed and train you every day. We'll be best friends."

"The gates won't hold for long," says Owlette. "If everything flies at HQ at once, it could knock it right over."

"Owlette, we'll hold the gates while you go inside HQ and turn off the beam," says Catboy.

But that isn't going to be so easy. The doors to HQ are magnetized shut.

Luckily, Birdy has a plan. Birdy finds Luna Girl and leads her right back to HQ and into one of the Luna Beams. Luna Girl's Luna Magnet cancels out the beam, and Birdy is able to get into HQ and grab the Luna Crystals. The Luna Beams turn off!

"I'll get you next time, PJ Pests," says Luna Girl.

"Birdy and I will be waiting for you," says Owlette.

The next day Connor, Greg, and Amaya go to the park. Greg brings Lionel, and Owlette brings Birdy.

"Let's see what you can do," Owlette says to Birdy.

Birdy does a loop-de-loop and lands . . . right on Greg's head.

"And sit, and stay," says Amaya as everyone laughs.